Dear Parents:

Congratulations! Your child is taking the first steps on an exciting journey. The destination? Independent reading!

STEP INTO READING® will help your child get there. The program offers five steps to reading success. Each step includes fun stories and colorful art or photographs. In addition to original fiction and books with favorite characters, there are Step into Reading Non-Fiction Readers, Phonics Readers and Boxed Sets, Sticker Readers, and Comic Readers—a complete literacy program with something to interest every child.

Learning to Read, Step by Step!

Ready to Read Preschool–Kindergarten
• big type and easy words • rhyme and rhythm • picture clues
For children who know the alphabet and are eager to begin reading.

Reading with Help Preschool–Grade 1
• basic vocabulary • short sentences • simple stories
For children who recognize familiar words and sound out new words with help.

Reading on Your Own Grades 1–3
• engaging characters • easy-to-follow plots • popular topics
For children who are ready to read on their own.

Reading Paragraphs Grades 2–3
• challenging vocabulary • short paragraphs • exciting stories
For newly independent readers who read simple sentences with confidence.

Ready for Chapters Grades 2–4
• chapters • longer paragraphs • full-color art
For children who want to take the plunge into chapter books but still like colorful pictures.

STEP INTO READING® is designed to give every child a successful reading experience. The grade levels are only guides; children will progress through the steps at their own speed, developing confidence in their reading.

Remember, a lifetime love of reading starts with a single step!

Step into Reading, Random House, and the Random House colophon are registered trademarks of Penguin Random House LLC.

Visit us on the Web!
StepIntoReading.com
rhcbooks.com

Educators and librarians, for a variety of teaching tools, visit us at RHTeachersLibrarians.com

ISBN 978-0-7364-4195-7 (trade) — ISBN 978-0-7364-9003-0 (lib. bdg.)
ISBN 978-0-7364-4196-4 (ebook)

Printed in the United States of America   10 9 8 7 6 5 4 3 2 1

Random House Children's Books supports the First Amendment and celebrates the right to read.

MAY 1 7 2021

DISNEY · PIXAR

LUCA

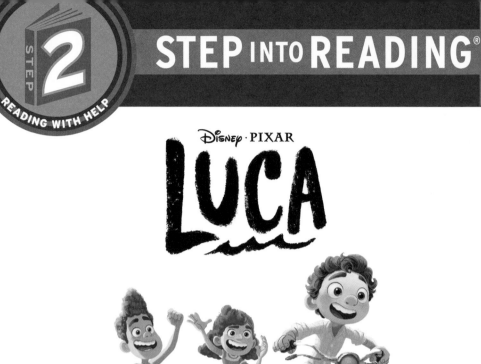

Friends Are Forever

adapted by Natasha Bouchard

illustrated by the Disney Storybook Art Team

Random House 🏠 New York

What are friends?
Friends are special.
Luca and Alberto
are friends.
They are
sea monsters!

Friends are fun.
Luca and Alberto
build and ride
a scooter.

The two friends
have an amazing
time together!

Friends are exciting!
Luca and Alberto have
a thrilling adventure
in a beautiful seaside
town called Portorosso.

Friends are different.

Giulia is not like
Luca and Alberto.
She is not
a sea monster.
She is a human girl.

Friends are brave.

Giulia stands up
for her friends.
She protects them
from a bully
named Ercole.

Friends are supportive.

Luca learns how
to ride a bicycle.
It is not easy at first.
But his friends
cheer him on.

Friends inspire.

Giulia points
to the train that is
headed to her school.
She tells Luca that
he can go to school, too.

Friends are ready
to help.

Alberto is trapped.

But Luca is there.

He is ready

to rescue Alberto.

Friends are loyal.
When Giulia gets hurt,
Luca and Alberto
go back for her.

Luca and Alberto are
the Portorosso Cup
champions!
The three friends
make a great team.